ASTERIX
THE GLADIATOR

TEXT BY GOSCINNY

DRAWINGS BY UDERZO

TRANSLATED BY ANTHEA BELL AND DEREK HOCKRIDGE

BROCKHAMPTON PRESS

PUBLISHERS OF ASTERIX IN OTHER LANGUAGES

Belgium	Editions du Lombard, 1–11 avenue Paul Henri Spaak, Brussels 7
Brazil	Editorial Bruguera LTDA, Rio de Janeiro, Rua Filomena Nunes 162
Denmark	Gutenberghus Bladene, Vögnmagergade 11, 1148 Copenhagen
Finland	Sanoma Osakeyhtio, Frotto Jankatu, Helsinki
France	Dargaud Editeur S.A., 12 rue Blaise-Pascal, 92 Neuilly-sur-Seine
Germany	Ehapa Verlag GmbH, Postfach 1215, 7 Stuttgart 1
Holland	Amsterdam Boek, Nassauplein 3, Haarlem
Italy	Arnoldo Mondadori Editore, Via GB Bodoni 1, 37100 Verona
Norway	Hjemmet Forlag (Gutenberghus Group), Frysjaveien 42, Oslo 8
Portugal	Livrario Bertrand, Ruo Joao de Deus, Venda Nova Amadora
Spain	Editorial Bruguera S.A., Camps y Fabres 5, Barcelona 6
Sweden	Hemmets Journal Forlag (Gutenberghus Group), Fack, 2022 Malmö 3

ISBN 0 340 10479 1 (cased edition)
ISBN 0 340 18320 9 (paperbound edition)

First published in Great Britain 1969
by Brockhampton Press Ltd, Salisbury Road, Leicester
Seventh impression 1974 (cased edition)
Second impression 1974 (paperbound edition)
Copyright © 1964 Dargaud S.A.
English-language text copyright © 1969 Brockhampton Press Ltd
Printed in Belgium by Henri Proost & Cie, Turnhout

GAULISH VILLAGE

COMPENDIUM

LAUDANUM

AQUARIUM

TOTORUM

ARMORICA

BELGICA

LUTETIA

SPQR

GAUL
(ROMAN CONQUEST)
50 B.C.

CELTICA

AQUITANIA

PROVINCIA

The year is 50 BC. Gaul is entirely occupied by the Romans. Well, not entirely… One small village of indomitable Gauls still holds out against the invaders. And life is not easy for the Roman legionaries who garrison the fortified camps of Totorum, Aquarium, Laudanum and Compendium…

a few of the Gauls

Asterix, the hero of these adventures. A shrewd, cunning little warrior; all perilous missions are immediately entrusted to him. Asterix gets his superhuman strength from the magic potion brewed by the druid Getafix...

Obelix, Asterix's inseparable friend. A menhir delivery-man by trade; addicted to wild boar. Obelix is always ready to drop everything and go off on a new adventure with Asterix – so long as there's wild boar to eat, and plenty of fighting.

Getafix, the venerable village druid. Gathers mistletoe and brews magic potions. His speciality is the potion which gives the drinker superhuman strength. But Getafix also has other recipes up his sleeve...

Cacofonix, the bard. Opinion is divided as to his musical gifts. Cacofonix thinks he's a genius. Everyone else thinks he's unspeakable. But so long as he doesn't speak, let alone sing, everybody likes him...

Finally, Vitalstatistix, the chief of the tribe. Majestic, brave and hot-tempered, the old warrior is respected by his men and feared by his enemies. Vitalstatistix himself has only one fear; he is afraid the sky may fall on his head tomorrow. But as he always says, 'Tomorrow never comes.'

THE ROMAN CAMP OF COMPENDIUM IS IN A FERMENT. THE PREFECT OF GAUL, ODIUS ASPARAGUS, IS PAYING A CALL ON CENTURION GRACCHUS ARMISURPLUS. THE PREFECT ARRIVES FROM THE NEARBY COAST WHERE HIS GALLEY HAS PUT IN...

PRESENT... PILUM!...

AVE, PREFECT! THIS IS A GREAT HONOUR FOR ME!

AVE, CENTURION! YOU'RE TELLING ME!

AND NOW FOR THE PURPOSE OF MY VISIT, CENTURION! I'M GOING TO ROME ON LEAVE, AND CUSTOM DECREES THAT I TAKE CAESAR A HANDSOME PRESENT... SOMETHING UNUSUAL AND VERY VALUABLE...

... I DID THINK OF TAKING HIM A PRESENT FROM LUTETIA, MAYBE A MARBLE MEMO TABLET FOR HIM TO CARVE DOWN HIS APPOINTMENTS, BUT THAT'S TOO ORDINARY...

THEN I HAD A BRILLIANT IDEA! WHY NOT TAKE CAESAR ONE OF THE INVINCIBLE GAULS FROM HEREABOUTS?

WHAT?!

BUT, PREFECT, ABOUT THESE INVINCIBLE GAULS ... THERE'S JUST ONE SNAG!

WELL, WHAT IS IT?

THEY HAPPEN TO BE INVINCIBLE!

THAT'S WHAT MAKES THEM SO VALUABLE! GET ME ONE OF THESE GAULS, AND YOU WON'T REGRET IT!

THERE'S CERTAINLY ONE WHO'S A BIT MORE HARMLESS THAN THE OTHERS... CACOFONIX THE BARD. HE OFTEN GOES FOR WALKS IN THE FOREST BY HIMSELF, LOOKING FOR INSPIRATION!

EXCELLENT! I MUST HAVE THIS BARD-AND FAST!

AND IN THE GAULISH VILLAGE...

GOODBYE, ASTERIX, I'M GOING FOR A WALK IN THE FOREST!

GOODBYE, CACOFONIX!

7

O VITALSTATISTIX, OUR BARD CACOFONIX HAS DISAPPEARED!

YOU'RE JUST SAYING THAT TO PLEASE ME...

THE ROMANS HAVE CAPTURED HIM!

WHAT?

BY TOUTATIS! EVEN IF IT IS A FUNNY IDEA OF THE ROMANS, THAT'S NOT PLAYING FAIR! WE CAN'T HAVE THIS SORT OF THING!

A GAUL MUST KNOW HOW TO MAKE HIS ENEMY RESPECT HIM! WE SHALL ORGANIZE A PUNITIVE EXPEDITION! LET THE DRUID PREPARE THE MAGIC POTION!

SOON AFTERWARDS THE GAULISH WARRIORS ARE DRINKING THE MAGIC POTION WHICH GIVES THEM INVINCIBLE STRENGTH...

NO, OBELIX! NOT YOU! I'VE ALREADY TOLD YOU YOU DON'T NEED ANY POTION! YOU'RE STRONG ENOUGH AS YOU ARE!

WHAT, ME STRONG? NOT A BIT OF IT! I'M AS WEAK AS ANYTHING!

GO ON! I'LL GIVE YOU THIS NICE MENHIR!

NO, NO, AND FOR THE THIRD TIME NO!

SILENCE! OUR CHIEF VITALSTATISTIX IS GOING TO MAKE A SPEECH!

FRIENDS, GAULS, COUNTRYMEN! WE MUST GIVE THESE ROMANS A GOOD LESSON, BY TOUTATIS!

AND REMEMBER, WE HAVE NOTHING TO FEAR BUT THE SKY FALLING ON OUR HEADS!

IN THE ROMAN CAMP OF COMPENDIUM THE TROOPS HAVE BEEN ALERTED...

AND REMEMBER, ROMANS, WE HAVE NOTHING TO FEAR BUT THE GAULS!

3-62

THE BATTLE IS SHORT...

BANG!
CLINKCLANKCLONK!
BIFF!

BUT SHARP...

SWOOOSH!

I CAN'T FIND CACOFONIX ANYWHERE... AH, THERE'S THE ROMAN COMMANDER!

BANG!
BING!

I SHALL FIGHT TO THE DEATH!

WANT ME TO THUMP YOU?

OH ALL RIGHT! ALL IS LOST! I SURRENDER! ALEA JACTA EST!

AND LET IT BE A LESSON TO YOU! NOW, GIVE US BACK OUR BARD, AND DON'T DO IT AGAIN!

THE FACT IS... YOUR BARD ISN'T HERE ANY MORE. AT THIS MOMENT HE'S ON BOARD A GALLEY, SAILING FOR ROME TO BE GIVEN TO CAESAR AS A PRESENT...

!!!

WE'RE WASTING OUR TIME...

A PRESENT? THAT'S A REALLY FUNNY IDEA!

LOOK AT THIS, ASTERIX! I'M SURE I'VE WON OUR BET! AND ONE LEGIONARY WAS FIGHTING BARE-HEADED TOO. IT'S AGAINST ALL THE RULES OF WARFARE TO GO INTO BATTLE IMPROPERLY DRESSED! I'VE A GOOD MIND TO REPORT HIM!

THE GAULS WITHDRAW, LEAVING BEHIND THEM THE AFTERMATH OF BATTLE...

THEY REALLY LET US HAVE IT, EH, SIR?

IN THE FIRST PLACE, GET THIS CAMP BACK INTO ORDER!!! WHAT'S ALL THIS UNTIDINESS IN AID OF? AND DON'T ANYONE EVER MENTION THIS BATTLE TO ME AGAIN!!!

NOW TO STOP THIS SHIP SAILING ALONG THE COAST!

ASTERIX AND OBELIX MAKE THE ANCIENT GAULISH SIGN INDICATING A WISH TO BE TAKEN ON BOARD... NOTE THE FOUR CLENCHED FINGERS AND THE THUMB JERKED IN THE DESIRED DIRECTION. IF YOU WISH TO GO TO ROME, THE DIRECTION OF THE THUMB IS IMMATERIAL, SINCE ALL ROADS LEAD THERE

N.B. THIS GESTURE IS STILL EMPLOYED TODAY, THOUGH NOT OFTEN TO STOP SHIPS

IT'S A PHOENICIAN GALLEY. THE PHOENICIANS ARE FAMOUS SAILORS AND MERCHANTS!

WHAT'S THE PHOENICIAN FOR SINGULARIS PORCUS?

WE'RE FROM TYRE IN PHOENICIA. MY NAME IS EKONOMIKRISIS. WOULD YOU LIKE TO BUY ANY GLASS, JEWELS, TEXTILES, PURPLE, FURNITURE?

NO, WE WANT TO GO TO ROME

HM...ER...ALL RIGHT, COME ON BOARD!

ARE THOSE SLAVES?

OH NO, THEY'RE PARTNERS... WHEN WE FLOATED THE COMPANY, I DREW UP THE CONTRACT AND THEY FAILED TO READ IT CAREFULLY BEFORE SIGNING. I'M CHAIRMAN AND MANAGING DIRECTOR

IT'S KIND OF YOU TO TAKE US TO ROME. I HOPE IT DOESN'T MEAN GOING OUT OF YOUR WAY?

AS IT HAPPENS, WE WERE PLANNING TO GO TO ROME. ONE OF MY PREDECESSORS ABANDONED HIS SHIP THERE...

IT SANK?

NO, HE SOLD IT. HE WAS A BETTER SALESMAN THAN SAILSMAN

A SAIL ON THE HORIZON, MR. CHAIRMAN!

IT MUST BE PIRATES! THEY MAY TAKE US PRISONER, KILL US, OR EVEN WORSE STEAL OUR MERCHANDISE!

SURE ENOUGH, ON BOARD THE PIRATE GALLEY...

SHIVER ME TIMBERS, WE'VE GOT 'EM, ME HEARTIES! PULL AWAY! THAT HEAVY PHOENICIAN SHIP WITH ALL ITS CARGO WILL NEVER ESCAPE US!

WE GONNA BO'D DEM, SAH!

TEEHEE HEE!

MY DEAR FELLOW DIRECTORS, I THINK WE SHALL BE OBLIGED TO FIGHT...

NO, NO, MR. CHAIRMAN! OUR CONTRACT SAYS WE HAVE TO ROW, BUT THERE'S NOTHING IN THE SMALL PRINT ABOUT FIGHTING!

NOW, I SUGGEST WE CHANGE THE CONTRACT. I HAVE AN IMPORTANT MODIFICATION TO MAKE

ME TOO!

ME TOO!

ME TOO!

ME TOO!

ME TOO!

ME TOO!

ME TOO!

WE CAN'T COUNT ON THESE CHATTER-BOXES TO FIGHT. WE'LL HAVE TO DEAL WITH THIS ON OUR OWN

GOODY! THERE'LL BE MORE ROOM! LOOK, HERE COME THE PIRATES. POOR THINGS!

THEY'RE WEARING HELMETS! WE CAN HAVE ANOTHER BET LIKE WE DID WITH THE LEGIONARIES!

+34

GIDDY GOAT'S HORNS, WE'LL MAKE JUST ONE MOUTHFUL OF THEM!

VANITAS VANITATUM ET OMNIA VANITAS!

WE MIGHT ON THE ONE HAND HOLD AN EXTRAORDINARY GENERAL MEETING TO DISCUSS TERMS OF CONTRACT, WHILE ALTERNATIVELY, ON THE OTHER HAND...

WELL, I THINK THIS WOULD BE A VERY GOOD MOMENT TO...

11

YOU HAVE SAVED WHAT IS DEAREST TO OUR HEARTS — OUR CARGO! NOW WE'RE BOSOM FRIENDS!

I ORIGINALLY INTENDED TO SELL YOU AS SLAVES WHEN WE CALLED AT THE NEXT PORT. BUT NOW I'LL TAKE YOU TO ROME AS AGREED

YOU CERTAINLY DO HAVE BUSINESS ACUMEN!

WHAT CAN YOU EXPECT? AS I WAS SAYING TO MY PARTNERS, WE'RE ALL IN THE SAME BOAT, AND WE MUSTN'T REST ON OUR OARS IF OUR OVERHEADS ARE NOT TO MAKE US GO UNDER!

MEANWHILE, IN ROME...

AVE, CAESAR!

AVE, ODIUS ASPARAGUS, PREFECT OF GAUL

HERE'S MY PRESENT, O CAESAR! A GAULISH BARD FROM THE TRIBE OF INDOMITABLE GAULS IN THE COMPENDIUM AREA

I'VE BEEN BROUGHT HERE AS A SOUVENIR... JUST AS IF I WAS A VULGAR PAINTED SHELL!

A BARD? HOW INTERESTING!

YOU CAN WAIT TILL THE COWS COME HOME BEFORE I'LL SING FOR YOU... AND YOU DON'T KNOW WHAT YOU'RE MISSING!

THANKS FOR THIS ORIGINAL LITTLE PRESENT, PREFECT. YOU MAY GO!

SEND FOR CAIUS FATUOUS, THE LANISTA *

SNAP!

* TRAINER OF THE GLADIATORS

CAIUS FATUOUS, CAN YOU MAKE A GLADIATOR OF THIS BARD?

DEAR ME, NO, O CAESAR! HE'S TOO WEAK... NOT ENOUGH MEAT ON HIM

IF I WASN'T RESTRAINING MYSELF...

VERY WELL THEN, THROW HIM TO THE LIONS AT THE NEXT GAMES. TAKE HIM AWAY!

WELL, SO WE'VE GOT A DATE AT INSTANTMIX'S PLACE THIS EVENING. WHAT DO WE DO TILL THEN?

WE COULD GO BACK AND HAVE SOME MORE BOAR?

BOAR ON THE SPIT

THE BATHS! I'VE OFTEN HEARD ABOUT THE ROMAN BATHS! LET'S GO AND HAVE A BATH!

THERMAE

GO AND GET UNDRESSED IN THE APODYTERIA

THAT MUST MEAN THE CHANGING ROOM...

THIS WAY, NOBLE LORDS!

IS IT US HE MEANS?

APODYTERIA

WE HAVEN'T GOT MUCH ON. I HOPE WE DON'T CATCH COLD!

SUDATORIA

IT'S HOT IN HERE!

I WONDER IF WE COULD OPEN A WINDOW

LOOK, CAIUS FATUOUS! YOU'RE ALWAYS ON THE LOOKOUT FOR GLADIATORS — WHAT DO YOU THINK OF THOSE TWO MEN?

INTERESTING. ESPECIALLY THE FAT ONE

CALDARIUM

LET'S TRY IN HERE... IT MAY BE COOLER

THIS WAS A FUNNY IDEA OF YOURS, ASTERIX, BY TOUTATIS!

HE SAID, 'BY TOUTATIS'... THEY'RE GAULS...

WE MAY BE HARD-BOILED, BUT THIS IS OVERDOING IT!

YOU SEEM TO BE STRANGERS HERE. I'LL GUIDE YOU ROUND THE BATHS. I COME HERE REGULARLY FOR MY HEALTH, THOUGH IT IS A BIT OF A SWEAT...

YOU SHOULD GO TO THE FRIGIDARIUM AND DIVE INTO THE POOL OF ICY WATER

ICY WATER? I'M ON MY WAY!

WATCH ME DIVE, ASTERIX! WATCH ME DIVE!

16

21

LET'S TRY A FEW CRAFTY QUESTIONS ON THIS GUARD. WE MUSTN'T AROUSE HIS SUSPICIONS...

NO...

HEY, YOU! WHERE'S CACOFONIX IMPRISONED?

?!

CELL XVIII FIRST BASEMENT DOWN, BUT IT'S A SECRET!

THERE!

SOON AFTERWARDS...

AND NOW FOR THE CIRCUS. I'LL DRINK A LITTLE MAGIC POTION

HERE'S MY PLAN— WE KNOCK DOWN EVERYONE AND EVERYTHING UNTIL WE FIND CACOFONIX AND THEN WE MAKE OFF WITH HIM!

THAT'S A CLEVER PLAN!

HALT! NO...

ENTRY!

CELL XV... CELL XVI... CELL XVII... WE'RE GETTING WARM!

OUR BET ABOUT THE HELMETS IS STILL ON, ISN'T IT?

CELL XVIII IS EMPTY!

HEY! WHAT ARE YOU TWO DOING HERE?

POP!

21

GRAND CIRCUS
GAMES
IMPRESARIO, CAIUS FATUOUS

CHARIOT RACES
GAULISH BARD
THROWN TO THE LIONS
GLADIATORIAL CONTESTS
WITH
ASTERIX
& OBELIX
THE INDOMITABLE GAULS
(BOOKING OFFICE NOW OPEN)

TIME PASSES BY, AND THE GLADIATORS ARE PUTTING ON WEIGHT...

MY FIRST IS A HUNDRED, MY SECOND IS A SIGN OF THE ZODIAC, MY THIRD IS A HIBERNIAN, MY FOURTH IS THE EGYPTIAN GOD OF THE SUN AND JULIUS CAESAR LOVES MY WHOLE! WHO AM I?

WHILE CAIUS FATUOUS IS LOSING IT...

THERE THEY GO AGAIN! PLAYING IDIOTIC GAMES INSTEAD OF TRAINING! A FINE CIRCUS THIS IS GOING TO BE!

IT'S C, LEO, PAT, RA... CLEOPATRA!

THAT WAS A DIFFICULT ONE THAT WAS!

THE GAMES ARE FIXED FOR TOMORROW. THIS WILL BE YOUR LAST NIGHT IN THE CIRCUS, YOU USELESS LOT!

WE DON'T REALLY WANT TO FIGHT ANY MORE, ASTERIX

DON'T WORRY! I PROMISE YOU WON'T HAVE TO RISK YOUR LIVES IN THE ARENA!

AND A VERY RELAXED GROUP OF GLADIATORS ARRIVES AT THE CIRCUS...

HA, HA! HO, HO!

STOP PUSHING, WILL YOU!

PORPUS IS A BEAST! PASS IT ON!

WHAT'S THE MATTER WITH THEM?

NO IDEA. LOCK THEM UP DOWN BELOW!

PORTER, WE WANT TO SEE OUR FRIEND CACOFONIX THE BARD

I'M NOT A PORTER AND YOU CAN'T!

VERY WELL THEN, WE SHALL TEAR OUT THESE BARS ONE BY ONE UNTIL YOU CO-OPERATE!

GO AHEAD AND TRY!

PLINNNK!

PLONNNK!

PLUNNNK!

STOP! LEAVE THE FIXTURES ALONE!

AH, ABOUT TIME TOO! WHAT SERVICE!

A HUGE CROWD IS FORMING OUTSIDE THE CIRCUS...

WASH YOUR TOGAS IN *SUPER PERSIC!* SUPER PERSIC WASHES EVEN PURPLER!

SCORE CARD! SCORE CARD!

CUSHIONS! CUSHIONS!

CHIPOLATAE! CANES CALIDI! CHIPOLATAE!

AND INSIDE THE IMPOSING ARENA THE TRUMPETS ANNOUNCE THE ARRIVAL OF CAESAR IN THE IMPERIAL BOX...

TANTAN TARA!!!!

PANEM ET CIRCENSES

LONG LIVE CAESAR!

CAESAR FOR EVER!

EVERYONE APPLAUDS THE DICTATOR...

CLAP! CLAP! CLAP! CLAP! CLAP! CLAP!

ET TU BRUTE!*

CLAP! CLAP! CLAP!

* YOU TOO, BRUTUS!

THAT BRUTUS... I CAN SEE I'M GOING TO HAVE TROUBLE WITH HIM *

CLAPCLAP! CLAP CLAP! CLAPCLAP! CLAPCLAP!

* AN EXAMINATION OF ACT III, SCENE 1 OF JULIUS CAESAR BY WILLIAM SHAKESPEARE WILL INDICATE THE PROPHETIC NATURE OF THIS REMARK

THIS WILL BE A GREAT SHOW, O CAESAR!

I HOPE SO, CAIUS FATUOUS. IF NOT, YOU'LL BE IN ON THE ACT

LET THE GAMES BEGIN!

GULP!

34

41

SO YOU WANT TO SEE SOME FIGHTING, ROMAN? THEN YOU SHALL! SEND IN SOME OF YOUR CRACK LEGIONARIES. MY FRIEND OBELIX AND I WILL DEAL WITH THEM. LEAVE THOSE OTHER POOR DEVILS ALONE!

OH, SO YOU WANT TO MAKE FUN OF ME, GAULS? VERY WELL! **SEND IN A COHORT OF MY BEST LEGIONARIES!!!**

THE REST OF YOU GO AND PLAY OUTSIDE...

YES, BUT WAS I OUT OR NOT?

I'LL JUST FINISH OFF THE MAGIC POTION...

SHALL WE DO THE HELMET ROUTINE AGAIN? SHALL WE, ASTERIX?

WELL, ARE THEY COMING OR DO WE HAVE TO GO AND FETCH THEM?

GOODY! HERE THEY COME, ALL WITH THEIR TIN HATS ON!

LEFT, RIGHT LEFT, RIGHT LEFT, RIGHT LEFT, RIGHT LEFT, RIGHT

UNARMED! I WANT TO PROLONG THE PLEASURE! I WANT TO SEE YOU FLATTEN THESE TWO GAULS WITH YOUR BARE HANDS!

I PROTEST! IT WON'T BE A FAIR FIGHT IF THEY'RE UNARMED!

BOING!

BONG! BANG! BING!

YOU COMING? I'VE STARTED ALREADY!

40

... AND FINALLY I ASK YOU TO FREE THE GLADIATORS. THEY'RE GIVING UP THEIR BLOODTHIRSTY JOB!

GRANTED, O GAUL!

MMPH? IS THE SHOW OVER YET?

I ASK YOU TO FREE THE BARD WE CAME TO RESCUE, AND LET US GO HOME TO GAUL BEFORE WE HAVE TO BEAT YOUR ARMY UP AGAIN ...

AND I HAVE ONE LAST FAVOUR TO ASK YOU, JULIUS ...

YOU SAW THAT? NOT A BAD PROGRAMME, EH?

LEND US CAIUS FATUOUS THE GLADIATOR TRAINER FOR OUR JOURNEY BACK TO GAUL. WE'LL SEND HIM BACK BY RETURN

GRANTED, BY JUPITER!

BUT... BUT ...

WHAT ARE YOU GOING TO DO WITH ME?

WE'RE GOING TO TEACH YOU A LITTLE LESSON, BY BELENOS!

LONG LIVE THE GAULS! LONG LIVE THE GLADIATORS! LONG LIVE CAESAR!

WHAT HAPPENED TO ME?

EXACTLY WHAT WILL HAPPEN AGAIN IF YOU DARE SING A NOTE BEFORE WE GET BACK TO GAUL!

NO FEAR! I'M NOT SINGING FOR ANY MORE ROMAN BARBARIANS, AND MOREOVER I'M TAKING NO FURTHER INTEREST IN THE MATTER!

HEY, WHERE ARE THE RUINS? DIDN'T A HOUSE FALL ON ME?

47

AT LAST WE HEAR THE LONG AWAITED SHOUT...

GAUL!!!

HURRAH, BY TOUTATIS!

THANKS FOR THE TRIP, EKONOMIKRISIS. PROMISE TO TAKE THE ROMAN HOME SAFE AND SOUND AND NOT SELL HIM ON THE WAY!

WHAT, SELL A PARTNER?

A FRIEND?

WE'RE VERY FOND OF CAIUS FATUOUS. HE KEEPS US ALL GOING!

RIGHT... OFF WE GO, PARTNER! LET'S SPEED OUR ENTERPRISE ON ITS WAY!

THE GAULISH VILLAGE CELEBRATES THE RETURN OF ITS HEROES WITH A GREAT FEAST... AND BUT FOR THE FACT THAT CACOFONIX WAS THE INVOLUNTARY VICTIM OF A TECHNICAL HITCH, HE WOULD CERTAINLY HAVE GIVEN THEM A SONG...

the end

proost Turnhout (Belgium)

PRINTED IN BELGIUM